Thunder in the Rumble Seat

Thunder in the Rumble Seat

KARL CONNELL

PUBLISHED BY FIDELI PUBLISHING, INC.

Cover art by Sandra Paniccia

Other Works by Karl Connell

Financing a Theatrical Production, Act II
Federal Legal Publications, 1964.

Wintoon
Privately Published, 1993.

Tularosa
Privately Published, 1998.

Biography of an Inventor, Dr. Karl Connell
Wintoon Waters, 2008.

Burr, Clinton and the Falls of General Benjamin Hovey
Fideli Publishing, Inc., 2013

Acknowledgements

Special thanks to Sandra Paniccia for the terrifying cover. She has shivered the 1937 Packard Rumble Seat Coupe with thunder — even though it would have been easier to draw a lightning bolt, which would not be true to the story.

Also thanks to my editor, Chuck Mason, who suggested that the main character needed to be introduced and made many other editorial corrections.

Sean Casey, an Actuary, has been most forthcoming with information about that profession; any errors about the profession are mine.

Special thanks for Jeannette Boucher for her encouragement and Karen Rosenstein for her proof reading and editorial assistance.

Also enjoy a laugh with Gene Blanchard and his watchdogs.

As always, Lawrence Fly Connell has corrected critical errors and provided salient suggestions.

Finally and most emphatically, the credit for the format and style of this work goes to Robin Surface, President of Fideli Publishing, Inc.

For Danielle, Mollie, Benjamin, Tabitha and Annabel.

Table of Contents

Introduction

ow long will I live? That is a question we all have. In fact, I remember lying in bed as a small boy in the late 1920s and wondering if I would see the year 2000.

The actuarial profession is devoted to this question. Sound actuarial advice is a key factor in the success or failure of many types of business. Probably life insurance comes first to mind. It is also vital in property/casualty insurance, health insurance, and pension plans. The advice must be grounded on a thorough knowledge of statistics, economics, business, mathematics and finance.

This story is about a fellow named George J. Foster. In his long career as an actuary, George had been consulted and given advice on what he thought was every type of business. Thus, he was surprised and intrigued when he received a telephone call to provide advice to the owners of a Continuing Care Retirement Community.

He did not know much about them, since these CCRCs were a fairly new phenomena. They replaced the back room where grandma sat in her rocking chair knitting scarves, sweaters, stockings and, most difficult, gloves for the grandchildren. They replaced the side porch where Grandpa whittled walking sticks and puffed on his corncob pipe. They also replaced the separate old folks homes and much maligned nursing homes, some reeking of Lysol, of yore.

He had heard discussions by some of his elderly friends. The kids had moved to California. They did not want to give up their furniture and their friendly neighbors to move to the opposite side of the continent.

Then he got in touch with one of his friends whose parents had moved to one of the newer CCRCs in the South. This friend was delighted his parents had made the move. He was told by his parents that it was like being in a tightly knit small town with many amenities. The apartments had modern, well-equipped kitchens, but Mom did not have to prepare dinner or change the sheets. The grounds were a gardener's delight, but Dad did not have to mow the lawn, weed the garden or empty the wastebaskets.

And, he added, it is fun to visit them at the convenient Guest Lodge, particularly if it is a long, snowy cold winter. He particularly liked the swimming pools and heated spa. But most of all, he did not have to worry about their care.

This is a story about what Foster found out when he accepted the assignment, and the long life he led until he saw a green flash at sunset.

CHAPTER ONE

The Actuary

George J. Foster was born to well off parents on November 14, 1930. His father was a Vice President of a national oil company and his socialite mother had attended Wellesley, one of the seven sisters leading women's colleges. But Foster was unlucky enough to be born with club feet. After several operations they were repositioned fairly well, but he never completely overcame an awkward limp.

He grew up in Greenwich, Connecticut, where his family had a handsome house with a spacious back lawn. He was sent to a local private day school, then to a prestigious private boarding school, St. Knowitall Academy. He spent six years there starting in the cubicles as a First Former and winding up as a prefect of the cubicles as a Sixth Former.

From the start he was kidded by some of the other boys for his limp. As a non-athlete, while others were playing football, hockey or baseball in the fall, winter and spring terms, he was assigned to the farm squad, and developed a lifelong aversion to pulling weeds out of the ground. He participated in debates and played on the chess team, but mostly concentrated on his studies.

The resulting high marks led to his acceptance to Harvard College. At Harvard he elected to major in statistics and won a prize for a thesis on suicide statistics. He graduated with honors in 1952.

After a number of dreary years of apprenticeship in the actuarial department of an insurance company, he wrote a treatise on death rates and founded his own consulting firm of actuaries. It was located in Stamford, Connecticut.

Several secretaries found him too difficult to work with and left shortly after being hired. Finally, he hired an attractive African-American woman named Penny Breed. She was quick with figures, an expert at soothing clients demanding instant attention, and she burnished his rough edges.

After many years of hard work he became recognized as an expert in his field and his reputation spread. He had enough work to hire a personable assistant, Buddy Allen, out of Rensselaer Polytechnic Institute. Indeed, he was elected a Vice President of the Society of Actuaries (SOA).

Accordingly, it was not surprising that he was called one day to consult with a private company controlled by the Pickering family in Chicago. This company owned and managed a dozen or so Continuing Care Retirement Communities. Foster was most intrigued with this engagement for three reasons, first because it was a new challenge, second he wanted to meet members of the remarkable Pickering family, and third to see the view from the 103rd floor of the Sears, now called Willis, Tower in Chicago in which their offices were located. Of course, he also needed the business.

As one of the six Vice Presidents of the SOA located in Schaumburg, Illinois, just northwest of Chicago, he had made many trips to the windy city. He caught an early morning flight from the convenient White Plains Airport, and landed in Chicago before twelve.

He had hoped to meet Peter Pickering, but instead was told to leave his overnight bag in the office and join a Mr. Robert Benny for lunch at the Metropolitan Club on the 63rd floor of the Tower. Although disappointed at not meeting one of the Pickerings, Foster straightened his tie and met Mr. Benny at his private table overlooking most of Chicago's waterfront on Lake Michigan. He found Benny to be an affable man, maybe a few years older than the comedian Jack Benny's perpetual age of 39.

After some small talk during a three-course lunch, Benny mentioned that Mr. Pickering would miss the meeting because he had been called to Washington to confer with the President of the United States. *Wow!* thought Foster, who had been most disappointed in the recent election of Bill Clint as President, *the Pickerings are involved with the Democrats.* He bit his tongue and changed the subject.

After dessert they moved to the conference room in the Pickering offices. That room was on the 78th floor. It lacked the waterfront view, but had a 20-foot conference table of polished black walnut. The celebrated dark chocolate grain of the wood was marred by a fine line at the center.

Benny laughed, "Old man Pickering didn't know there was no way to get a plank of wood this long and this wide to the 78th floor in one piece after the building was finished, so they had to saw it in half, but we are not here to talk about that mistake. A serious situation has arisen at one of our CCRCs on the west coast of Florida. The residents there are not dying on schedule! Let me explain."

"To be a Continuing Care Retirement Community you have to have an independent living section, an assisted living section, and a skilled nursing care facility. There are two types of CCRCs, the rental type and the insurance contract type. In the rental type you pay a reasonable rent for your apartment, and then much more if you move to assisted living or the care center. Now, our problem is with one of our insurance types named Packard Village in Southwest Florida."

Foster interrupted, "Yes, I looked it up on the internet before I flew out here. You can spend the rest of your life in a CCRC moving between levels as care is needed."

"Right," said Benny. "As an insurance type we make a careful demographic evaluation of applicants to be sure they pay enough in advance, say, anywhere between $200,000 and $1,000,000 to defray the extra expense should they need to move to Assisted Living or skilled nursing care in the Care Center. Many of them die while still in Independent Living. When they do, Mr. Pickering, the general partner, makes a bundle and can also make a nice distribution to our limited partners."

"What a business model," said Foster, "The quicker they die the more money you make, and then you re-rent their apartment. Do you own an adjacent funeral parlor? Do you really try to keep them alive?"

"You bet we do. We are required to do so by law; indeed they have a statutory Bill Of Rights." Benny replied. "Mr. Pickering even sends his daughter, Polly Pickering, sharp as a tack, down to Packard Village to see everything is run according to Hoyle.

"Of course, now that President Clint has appointed him to become the Secretary of the Treasury, he is putting all his holdings into a blind trust. I expect that the trustee will sell his interest in Packard Village to one of the limited partners.

"But to get back to the problem at hand, white men — we have very few people of color apply — are supposed to die at 78.8 years of age and women at 83.7. However, we only admit applicants that are at least 62. We have to take into account the fact that many of our applicants may already be in their seventies or eighties so we have to look up the life expectancy for people of their particular age."

Benny went on, "We picked up this property for a song. A Dr. Noah Packard and his two partners started this CCRC back in 1980. Dr. Packard was proud of his handsomely restored 1937 Packard Rumble Seat Coupe. He told his partners that since most of the residents of this new CCRC would be in the rumble seat of their life span, Packard Village would be an apt name. They agreed.

"They built a Clubhouse and ten buildings around a lake. They also built a care center and assisted living facilities crowded into one building. This did not meet the requirements of Florida Law. They tried to get a large enough construction loan to add the needed facilities, but failed. So with the approval of Peter Pickering, we bought out Dr. Packard and his partners, negotiated a construction loan and built a one hundred unit Assisted Living Residence and a one hundred bed Care Center.

"We put all the land and buildings into a Delaware corporation, Packard Village Holding Company. It receives 91% of the lump sum payments and 9% goes to run sales. The stock of the corporation is owned by a limited partnership, with Mr. Pickering the General Partner. The corporation leases the entire facility to a non-profit corporation for a nominal amount. We have 10 of the 12 board seats on the non-profit. It pays for the food, staff and all but the maintenance of the common buildings and medical facilities."

Foster was silent for a minute or two. He should have been paying attention, but the mention of a rumble seat had sent him into a reverie. The summer after he graduated from St. Knowitall, one of his roommates, Jake Blake, had invited him to dine with his pretty date, Susan, and her somewhat awkward looking kid sister, Sally. After dinner Jake drove them in a Model A Ford Coupe to the outdoor movie theatre outside Bridgeport. Jake and his date sat inside the Coupe while Foster and Sally sat in the rumble seat. Foster couldn't remember the movie but he sure would never forget two hours in the "rumble" seat with Sally. She turned out to be very nimble there.

"Let's go over that once more," said Foster. "You have three layers."

"Yes," said Benny. "Sometimes it gets contentious as to who pays for repairs," he said and he summarized the setup again.

"Thanks for your summary," said Foster, "but from what you have told me, even taking into account the excellent health care you are providing, I cannot fathom why your residents are not dying faster. You know what, I think the best way for me to give you some insight into what is going on is for me to go down to the facility itself. I'm well over 62 but with my lame leg and wrinkles, I look older than I am. Besides, I'd enjoy a few days at the beach."

Benny said, "I've got just the ticket for you. We have considered using one of our model apartments as a trial apartment. We could send you down there as our first trial applicant for two weeks."

It had flashed through Foster's mind that he was becoming a spy. He had always wondered what it would be like to be a spy. It appealed to him.

Benny and Foster then discussed and settled on a fixed fee for a two-week "trial" stay at Packard Village and a detailed actuarial report.

Foster did not set off for Florida immediately. He registered at the Trump International Hotel in Chicago, and spent several days commuting to the SAC offices, polishing off reports to other clients. He also stopped shaving and towards the end of the week finished his open reports at his hotel. He then shopped for a cane, bathing suit and other Florida clothes.

He booked a flight on United out of O'Hare direct to Southwest Florida Regional Airport. By the time he reached Florida he was hiding behind a scraggly beard and moustache. Although only in his late sixties, with his limp he could easily pass for being over eighty.

On arrival he caught a $55 taxi ride to Packard Village. The guard at the gate gave him a welcome package for new residents and the electronic keys to a second floor one-bedroom unit in Building One, the oldest in Packard Village. It had a pleasant view of Sunset Lake, which was enhanced by a small fountain. It had been comfortably furnished as a model unit. It had a working telephone and a television set. The bedroom had two single beds.

He freshencd up from the trip and noticed the tap on the sink was hard to shut off. Then he sat down to analyze the Directory included in his welcome packet. He noted that it was provided by the Patrons of Packard Village, whoever they were.

Before he could finish his analysis, it was dinnertime and he caught the 6 o'clock tram to the dining room, named the Chandelier Room. He stopped to wash his hands in the men's room. It was immaculate with a handsome tile floor. He was seated at a so-called joining table of six with one couple and three single ladies. The ladies were well groomed and welcomed him. One of them, Jean Smith, was also from Building One. He made a special effort to make her acquaintance.

The menu had a variety of choices. He selected lamb chops; the portion was a lavish rack, accompanied by enough mint jelly to coat his dinner plate green. They were excellent; medium rare just as he had requested.

After dinner, he returned to his analysis of the Directory. He noted there were 703 residents, 448 women and only 255 men. Of the 703 residents, 579 were in Independent Living, 83 in Assisted Living and 41 in the Care Center. There appeared to be 163 couples in Independent Living, two in Assisted Living and two in the Care Center. Taking the 167 couples mostly married from the total population, left only 88 unattached men for 281 unattached women — more precisely 3.2 single females for every single male!

Foster was, of course, familiar with the effect that widowhood — the death of one spouse — has on accelerating the death of the other. He speculated on why the lifetime of the residents exceeded the number of years predicted by the Mortality Tables. *Are most of the single women spinsters rather than widows?*

The next morning he was invited to tour the property by the sales department. His tour guide was Sylvia Johnson, an attractive young woman. She enthusiastically said how delighted she was to take the first "trial" applicant on a tour.

First she took him to the West Club House. It housed an English Pub, a deli restaurant, a gym and an auditorium. Beyond that she drove past the swimming pools, hot spa and tennis and croquet courts. She then drove around the par three golf course winding between buildings, palm trees and lakes.

Finally she stopped at Assisted Living and the Wellness Clinic in the Care Center. All the while she chatted about all the services provided including laundry, weekly cleaning and lawn care. Then, what a surprise, she offered him use of a stylish sales golf cart for the trial period. He gladly accepted, since driving one was such fun!

In a few days, Foster met Alice Bogle, the Executive Director of the Village. She was the only person there who knew he was a spy, not a genuine trial applicant. She was a good-looking woman with a clear grasp of her difficult job — to keep the Pickerings, the employees and the residents happy all at the same time. She gave him access to the confidential reports of the Packard personnel who interviewed applicants for admission.

He also invited his Building One friend, Jean, out to lunch. She was friendly enough but had a problem with being short of breath. They went to a seafood restaurant along a canal. Foster persuaded Jean to join him in a beer.

As they munched on Lobster Rolls, he steered the conversation to a run down on the other residents of Building One. She mentioned that Ken Cornwell on the first Floor was talking up perpetual life. He had recommended that the Packard Village Investment Club buy stock in a French Drug Company, Sanofi. This company had just acquired patent rights to a drug that might cause your cells to take you back to 30 years old. She said Ken had told her that there were already nine organisms that lived perpetually.

Foster returned to his apartment, ready to explore or explode the myth of perpetual life, when the phone rang. It was Benny. He was breathles. "I have just heard that the Trustee has agreed to sell the Pickerings' interest in Packard Village to one of our limited partners, Herbert George Guzman, who is also buying out all the other limited partners. Drop the project and deep six your notes. I don't want rumors of an actuarial anomaly to jinx the deal for Mr. Pickering."

"Okay," said Foster, "but what about my fee?"

"I've wired your full fee and a Confidentiality Agreement to the offices of Alfred & Strickright, our local counsel in Naples. When you sign, seal and deliver the Confidentiality Agreement, they'll hand you your check in current federal funds. Tell your acquaintances at Packard that you have to leave to help a sick relative. Sorry, but I have got to go." Brusquely Benny hung up.

It was still early afternoon, so Foster got Alfred & Stirckright on the phone, arranged an appointment for 9:30 the next morning, put on his bathing suit and finally made his trip to Barefoot Beach. It was beautiful, not too crowded, the waves modest, and although it was early November, the water temperature pleasant and the sun warm.

The next morning he signed the Confidentiality Agreement and handed it over against receipt of his check. He was able to catch the 11:49 a.m. Jet Blue flight to White Plains.

Ransoming his car from the short term parking garage where, expecting a short trip to Chicago, he had foolishly left it, Foster returned to his bachelor's apartment in Stamford.

Calling the office, he found Penny and Buddy had everything pretty well under control so he gave Helen Conway, his favorite bridge partner, a ring. She invited him to join her in New York City for the American Contract Bridge League's Eastern States Regional Tournament in a few weeks.

He accepted the invitation, but did not play up to his usual impeccable standards. He could not get the thought of perpetual life out of his mind. He did have one triumph at the tournament though, a Deschapelles Coup.

[For Bridge players only: A Deschapelles Coup is where a defender plays a sure winner in a suit, say a guarded King of Spades, to drive out the Ace of Spades in Dummy, the only entry to Dummy's long suit, say, Diamonds, before it has become established.]

Twice a Spy

Almost six months passed and he received a call from a Mr. Aaron Groom, who inquired whether he could meet Mr. Herbert George Guzman, now the sole stockholder of Packard Holding Company, the Delaware Corporation that owned the facilities at Packard Village. Business had been slow, but Foster had signed a Confidentiality Agreement, so he told Groom that he would have to review his pending assignments and would get back to him.

Foster called the esteemed Stamford law firm of Tuthill & Townsman and discussed the possible engagement with them. They asked for a copy of the Confidentiality Agreement to review. He sent it to them by a messenger service.

In a few days Stoddard Townsman himself called back. The matter was not free from doubt but they were inclined to believe, as long as he did not mention his previous service or make any mention of his findings, he could accept the assignment. To protect himself, Stoddard recommended that he obtain a formal written opinion of the firm, based on exhaustive research.

That jarred Foster into complaining over the phone: "Research! Research? I hired your firm because you are supposed to know the law, not to do research."

Stoddard pointed out that his firm carried a ten million dollar malpractice insurance policy; and even if its opinion was adjudged incorrect and Foster suffered financial loss as a result of relying on it, he could recoup the loss from the firm.

Mollified that he was really buying insurance, not paying for useless research, Foster dealt with another problem. Guzman might want him to visit the Village and if he did so, Guzman might find out about his aborted "trial" sortie as a spy.

Since Alice Bogle, the Executive Director, was the only one who knew anything about his soiree as a spy, he called her to discuss the matter. To his surprise, he learned she had left to accept a position as Vice President of a larger CCRC in the Midwest. She had been temporarily replaced by a man, Thomas Fletcher, the Assistant Executive Director. Mr. Fletcher did not have a clue that he had been there previously and turned him over to the sales associate he had met on his first trip, Sylvia Johnson.

Sylvia, whose telephone voice sparkled with enthusiasm for a share in the 9% commission, explained that he would have to pay $240,000 in advance for a Continuing Care Contract for a one-bedroom unit. Furthermore, he would have to pay $5,000 more if he wished to have a covered carport. This would license him to live in an attractive 1,000 square foot apartment consisting of a living room, bedroom, kitchen and bath with one large clothes and one small coat closet. However, the only vacancy at the moment was a model apartment in Building One that was already furnished, and there would be a $10,000 additional fee for the furniture.

So, despite some misgivings, he called Groom back and said he had managed to set aside other matters and could meet Mr. Guzman. He was told to meet Mr. Guzman at his New York City condominium on the 48th floor of the startling Trump Tower, using the private entrance on 56th Street just off Fifth Avenue.

Foster took the Amtrak early train to the city and, for once, it arrived on time — just short of one hour from

Stamford to Pennsylvania Station. A taxi ride brought him to the Trump Tower, with its plate glass walls, atrium, shops, waterfall and restaurants, before noon.

After a leisurely lunch, he was pressing the door chime to the Guzman condominium right on the dot of his two o'clock appointment. He was met at the door by a slim, dark haired woman in a tailored grey pants suit. She had arresting green eyes and eyelashes so long that it was hard to believe they were real.

She said "Mr. Foster?"

He nodded.

She continued, "I'm Barbara Baxter, Mr. Guzman's secretary. He's in a conference. Please be seated and he will be with you as soon as possible."

Before he sat down, a tall handsome fellow with brown eyes and wavy brown hair came into the room. Barbara Baxter blinked her green eyes and gave him an adoring smile, but he paid no attention to her. He said, "Hello, Mr. Foster. I'm Aaron Groom, Mr. Guzman's confidential assistant for our nine CCRCs. Mr. Guzman is on the phone." Foster wondered why they gave different reasons for the delay, but Groom went on.

He explained that all nine communities recently acquired by Guzman were of the insurance type. To join, applicants had to pay a whopping down payment and monthly fees as long as they lived. If they died when predicted by mortality tables, the owner could pocket most of the down payment. If they lived longer than predicted, the owner, now Mr. Guzman, would pocket a smaller percentage of the down payment.

Groom explained Mr. Guzman was disturbed because the residents of Packard Village had in the past died at the rate of five, six or seven a month, but in the six months that he had owned the place, the rate had slowed to two or three a month — a highly unprofitable rate.

Finally, Foster met Mr. Guzman in person. He was a short, rotund … well, fat, man with a reddish face and wavy dark hair flecked with white. He did not look like a billionaire, as he was rumored to be.

Shaking hands with Foster, he said, "Call me Herb and I'll call you George — that's my middle name so I can't forget it. I'm sorry to keep you waiting; I just received a very rare call from my only living grandchild, Gerald. He is a senior at Antioch College. You ever hear of it? It is out in Yellow Springs, Ohio."

Foster nodded, "I hear it is quite liberal."

"Too much so, in my opinion," said Guzman as he paused to light a cigarette, as though gathering his thoughts. Then he went on, "George, I believe the Trustee for old man Pickering has really pulled a fast one on me. My good friend, Sam Wallace, used to live in Chicago and introduced me to the Pickerings. He said they were straight shooters. They never told me that those folks down at Packard Village were not dying on schedule. I aim to find out why."

Foster then proceeded to give an extended lecture on generalized lifetime statistics, the different rates for men and women, the effects of a mate dying, and ethnic variances. He finally wound up, "Herb, the best way for me to get the low-down is to go south to Packard Village, spend two weeks there and get to the bottom of the aberration from normalcy. In a couple weeks, I can let my beard grow, drag my lame left foot a little more, go through the entrance interview and the whole nine yards."

"Okay, you'll be our spy," said Guzman, gleefully. "Work out the fee and scope of your report with Aaron."

With that, the brief interview was over and Foster and Groom retreated to the reception room to iron out the details. Groom explained that Mr. Guzman owned all the stock of Packard Holding Company and was Chairman of its six-man Board of Directors. He said the rest of the Board consisted of himself, Mr. Wallace, and Shawn, Bill and Thomas — three old golfing buddies of Mr. Guzman, who always voted as directed by Guzman. He added, "If you received $1,000 for each meeting, the use of a Cadillac and a week at the Doral Country Club in Miami to attend the annual meeting in January, how would you vote?"

Before parting, Foster asked, "Mr. Guzman mentioned he had only one living grandchild, has there been a recent death in the family?"

"You haven't heard?" asked Groom. "Guzman's wife, daughter, son-in-law and granddaughter were all headed to see the pyramids. They were all on that Egyptian airliner that crashed into the sea off Nantucket, killing all 217 persons aboard. They say the crash was intentionally caused by a revengeful Egyptian Army officer."

"Good, Lord, I read about that," said Foster, "No wonder he took the call."

After agreeing on a fee and arranging an advance for the down payment, which would come right back to Guzman's holding company, Groom was full of ideas on how to speed up the death rate. Why not admit more men? They died faster, particularly if you fed them fattening food. Foster had already learned in his brief stay that some of the men at Packard Village already had what they called "the Packard paunch," but caught himself before saying so and revealing he had already been there. After finalizing all the details with Groom, he returned to Stamford.

He called Sylvia Johnson, who greeted him like a long lost boyfriend, and then faxed a Continuing Care Contract to his office. It called for a substantial down payment, which he mailed off the next day. She told him that since he had been there the apartment had been used by several other applicants on a "trial" basis and that it would be thoroughly cleaned and refurbished by the beginning of the next month. That gave him what he thought was plenty of time to clean up uncompleted assignments, give Buddy Allen and Penny instructions, and grow his beard.

He had not anticipated the telephone calls he received from Groom almost daily. It was as though he had made a contribution to a candidate for President of the United States, after which the phone never stopped ringing for another contribution.

Groom kept harping on society's discrimination against men. He had come across a website listing 24 indicators of systemic discrimination against men. Life expectancy is seven years shorter for men. Men get longer sentences for spousal abuse than women. Women hold 65% of the country's wealth and so on and so on. Of course, this accounted in part for the reason that Packard Village had more women than men. Foster very much wished he had opted for an hourly fee and could charge a quarter hour for a five-minute phone call like most lawyers.

In June 1998, he again arrived at Packard Village. This time he rented a car at the airport and drove to Packard Village. At the gate, he was given the keys to Unit 222, its mailbox and storage closet, as well as a welcome packet containing a Resident Manual with 44 pages of rules and regulations.

He was directed to the Assisted Living Residence where he was given a physical. The nurse there remarked that he looked in very good shape for someone 82 years of age. He was glad he did not have to show his fraudulent birth certificate; he really did not like lying. He'd begun to lose his enthusiasm for spying; it was like a fly being caught in a spider's web — every lie led to another. He lugged his luggage up to Unit 222. He was pleased again by the pleasant view of the fountain in Sunset Lake.

Several of the Building One residents welcomed him back as the first "trial" applicant who had actually moved to Packard Village. A smiling lady, Sally Halbertson, dropped by and introduced herself as the Building Representative. She welcomed him, invited him to the monthly building dinner the next Monday and emphasized the importance of observing the recycling rules. She told him that his friend Jean had moved to Assisted Living.

Instead of relying on her for information, he made a point of getting involved in as many activities as possible himself to find out why the residents exceeded their statistical lifespan. One of their activities was The Patrons of Packard Village. The Patrons collected, sorted, cleaned, and sold for a song, discarded clothing, furniture and other household goods contributed by residents who had downsized or died. The Patrons used the proceeds to make improvements, such as the car wash, and to reward employees.

He also learned about the many activities sponsored by Lifestyle Enrichment, a fancy name for a social director. There were trips to the beach, exotic restaurants, the Philharmonic, zoo and botanical gardens. There were all kinds of card games, contract bridge, poker, even euchre and Mah Jong. There was painting by the art group, pottery and vase making by the ceramic group, yoga and tai chi classes, a well-equipped gymnasium, dancing classes, bible studies, book clubs and trivia games, not to mention sports such as bocce ball, croquet, tennis and golf.

With his limp, he was unable to infiltrate the tennis players or the golfers, but he did take a crack at croquet. When he grew up in Greenwich his family sometimes laid out a croquet court on the back lawn. In her long skirt, his mother taught him to hit the ball from his right side even though his right foot was the more twisted one. It was pretty easy to hit the smaller balls through the bigger hoops.

But here at Packard Village they played American six-wicket croquet. The wickets were much narrower than the back yard hoops in Greenwich. Furthermore, the ball was much bigger and the mallets weighed a ton. Besides, some of the players seemed to have a bit of a problem with short-term memory. They sometimes played out of turn or hit the wrong ball by mistake.

Also, there were often arguments about being awarded extra shots after hitting another ball. These are not allowed if you previously hit that ball, and thus became dead on it, unless you have cleared deadness by going through another wicket. This sometimes led to controversy.

When he mentioned this to Groom, Groom became as excited as a cat on a hot tin roof. "We have got to get more people playing Croquet. Constant controversy about deadness must shorten lives!" he crowed. "Don't they ever get wacked on the head by a mallet and die?"

Foster was lucky enough to join a men's group of eight that met for dinner every Thursday night. They had a vacancy because one of the regulars, Harry, was away on a honeymoon. Did anyone know the woman he had married? Yes, she was a widow called Betsy Youngling. Was she young? No. Was she good looking? Not really, perhaps she looked a little more like the Wicked Witch of the West than Ingrid Bergman. Was she rich, a youngling of the beer brewery with that name? Nobody knew for sure but she drove a Toyota, not a Lexus or Cadillac. Well, it must be, with Harry's dim eyesight, he was marrying her because she could drive at night!

One day Foster bumped into Ken Cornwall putting a trash bag in the garbage closet. He had heard that Ken had sued Packard Village and received a big award, and he wanted to get the details. So he asked Ken out to lunch.

They went to L'Auberge, a recently opened French restaurant he heard about at the men's table. Foster ordered a bottle of excellent Bordeaux. Over the Bordeaux Foster maneuvered the conversation around to confidentiality agreements. Finally, he said, "I hear you had a big settlement with Packard Village."

Ken said, "Like a lot of rumors that is incorrect." He went on, "You see Building One is between a lake and a slough. The slough fills up with water in the rainy season. Furthermore the tiny storm drain in front of the west entrance fills up with leaves and does not drain the water; it soon backs up and the water gets ankle deep. Then many little particles of a substance I have agreed to keep confidential float in the air.

"On a normal day here, there are 250,000 of these particles floating in each cubic liter of air. That number is perfectly safe, but if 5,000,000 are floating in each cubic liter in a building, the regulations promulgated by the Federal Occupational Safety and Health Administration require the building to be shut down until the number of these particles has been reduced to safe levels.

"When these older buildings at Packard were built, the living rooms were foreshortened to provide a spacious open screened lanai. If an applicant wanted a larger living room for five grand extra they would patch out the floor of the lanai. Sometimes water got under these patches and seeped into the apartment below. Besides there are two standards for maintenance here. If a repair is needed for anything the residents pay for out of their monthly rent, the maintenance people are Johnny on the Spot. But if it is something the owner's corporation has to pay for, such as a leaky hot water boiler, it is ignored or delayed, to keep within budget.

"When I was a young lawyer, in the early 1950s," Ken went on, "I worked for four years as litigation counsel for Pathe, a Motion Picture Laboratory and Film Distributor in New York City. Many of the films it distributed were Class B movies, the kind where Frances Langford sang songs and after a few bumps along the love trail, everything turned out happily ever after.

"Now, television had just become popular. Everyone bought a set and preferred seeing Milton Berle joke about his incompetent wife to seeing Frances Langford sing about her errant boyfriend. Nevertheless, Pathe tried to get these B films into as many theatres as possible, but the theatre owners turned Pathe down. As a result, the producers lost money and sued the distributor for failing to use its 'best efforts' to distribute the films. There were 40 of these suits pending, all with the same exact legal issue — had 'best efforts' been used. It was my job to see these suits never got to trial.

"Fortunately, the Civil Practice Rules permit endless motions for more discovery. When you won a motion for discovery, say, to depose an exhibiter who was exhorted but refused to play the film in Dubuque, Iowa, and it was granted, but followed with a similar motion to depose the exhibitor in Des Moines, Iowa, and it was denied, you would appeal and get another six-month delay.

"I found that Packard's counsel was pulling the same trick on me that I had played on the B film producers. He had filed six motions and had probably a dozen more pending. He wanted to depose the firm that had collected the air sample, then depose the Laboratory that tested it and so on and so on. I'd been there, done that. So, with too many particles still in my lungs to bother with extended litigation, I settled early for a relative pittance."

Although Ken held up his hand to stop, Foster poured Ken another glass of Bordeaux. Ken said, "All these pay in advance, continuing care communities face a very serious problem. As a member of the Packard Investment Club, I have subscribed to several of the stock tote services. They are mostly located in Baltimore, Maryland. They let you subscribe to their basic service for less than $50 a year, then they send you a long spiel about how their advice has made many very rich and then they tell you about a super stock that may increase a thousand or more fold but they will name it 'in just a moment.'

"The same guy must write for all of these touts. When he says 'in just a moment' he means he is about to extol how much money you will make for the next three or four hundred or even a thousand words and then ask you for four thousand dollars to subscribe to a special service that will name the alleged super stock. Once in a while, these services will actually recommend a stock for the basic service rate.

"One such stock, Sanofi, they claim holds patents on ways to cure aging, which they consider a curable disease. It claims our RNA, ribonucleic acid, wears out. RNA carries the information stem cells need to reproduce worn out cells in our body. If RNA wears out, it does not accurately transmit information for making the correct new cells. This tout claims that if you can get your RNA freshened up a bit, it will repair you back to age 30."

It seemed Ken would go on and on as long as the Bordeaux lasted, but Foster, who rarely had wine for lunch, had heard enough and was not about to invest in a second bottle.

When he returned to his apartment, he lay down for a nap, but couldn't go to sleep. Let's see, to go to sleep you were supposed to count sheep jumping over a fence. But instead of sheep, he drowsily saw hordes of lemmings jumping off a cliff into the sea. He had seen that once years before in a Pathe newsreel.

He then thought about how crowded tiny spaceship earth would be if men and women lived forever. What would happen to them? Then he thought about the "right to life" zealots who opposed abortion even in cases of rape. Maybe the Chinese were right, stop at one. Then he remembered a conversation he had once overheard between two women at the next table while waiting for a bridge game to start. One of them enthused about the perpetual life church she had joined. Was there really such a church? Was it about cryogenics, attaching Ted Williams frozen head to a new body and bringing back another .400 hitter?

He got up, washed his face, gargled and said to himself, "No more Bordeaux lunches."

CHAPTER THREE

Lanky Lucy

To clear his mind, he went out for a brisk walk around Sunset Lake. In the heat, he ran out of breath on the far side. He noticed a sign pointing to the dog park. As a shy youngster, he had implored his parents to buy him a dog. One Christmas he got his wish, an obedient Parson Russell Terrier he called Terry.

He followed the sign and entered the dog park, but there were no dogs there. He sat down alone on a pleasant bench in the shade under a gumbo-limbo tree with peeling red bark. Soon a tall lanky woman walking two dogs came by and asked if she could join him in the shade.

Foster said, "Certainly, I like dogs. What a cute pair of dogs you have. Are they Terriers?"

"Yes," she said with a trace of a slightly guttural foreign accent. "They are friendly Wire Fox Terriers."

He told her about his Parson Russell Terrier and they chatted about the traits of the many breeds of terriers. Noting one of her dogs had dark paws and the other light, he said, "Do you call them pepper and salt?"

"No," she said. "They are named Timex and Rolex."

Foster, a bit startled, said, "That seems like very strange names for dogs. Do they tick and tock?"

"Not at all," she said. "It is the exactly correct name because they are my watch dogs!"

Foster turned to take her in. She was a tall, nice-looking, long-legged lady, with a modest bosom, fairly flat belly and smooth complexion. She was dressed in a light green stylish pantsuit. It emphasized her long legs attractively. Really, she was quite good looking, fore and aft, but for one feature, an overly long, slightly squashed in nose. It reminded him of some people he had seen before, but he could not quite place them.

After finding out her name was Lucy Barksdale, and that she lived in Building Six across the Lake from Building One, and had moved to Packard Village fairly recently, he left her and Timex and Rolex.

During a restless night's sleep, it came to him. Her nose reminded him of some men and women he had seen before.

But he could not place them. Was he coming down with face blindness? Good Lord, had he been stricken with prosopagnosia? Wait a minute; her nose reminded him of a number of men and women he had seen in Luxembourg. Many carried a long, concave promontory on the front of the face through which to breathe. Thank goodness, he did not have prosopagnosia after all. In fact, he felt quite clever; he had a good memory of nosia!

Foster did not feel brash enough to call Lucy up and tell her of his supposition or mention her nose. Instead, the next afternoon, he shut down his laptop and took the same walk around the lake as the day before. This time, lanky Lucy had beat him to the bench under the gumbo-limbo tree.

An aeroplane flew overhead, and Timex and Rolex barked. Foster and Lucy segued into talking about adventures aloft and troubles with customs inspectors. That gave Foster the incident he was after. "You know, one time I was invited to visit my old prep school roommate Jake Blake. He had been appointed to be Ambassador of Luxembourg by President Nix just after Pearle Mesta left that post."

"Why I grew up in Luxembourg City," said Lucy, wiping a tear with her handkerchief.

Foster went on telling her about being met at the Customs Inspection Station by a Foreign Service Officer and how he felt triumphal as he was whisked through Customs in no time. They chatted some more and Foster asked her to join him the next day at L'Auberge, the new French restaurant where he had lunched with Ken Cornwall.

At the restaurant they were seated at an end table next to each other. She had left Timex and Rolex to watch over her apartment. Even though Lucy chose freshly caught pompano with lime dressing for lunch, calling for a white wine, Foster ordered the delectable red Bordeaux again.

They started talking about Luxembourg. "It was a terrible time, 1940," she said. "Mother died in the summer of 1939, just before World War II started with the Germans invading Poland. Then Dad became sick. We decided the best thing to do was to leave for York, England, where Dad had cousins.

"We started our trip just before the German Blitzkrieg through Luxembourg, Belgium and the Netherlands. It commenced on May 12, 1940. When we got to Dunkerque, its harbor was crowded with both naval and pleasure boats, and just about anything that floated, but only British soldiers were allowed to board the flotilla. They were reserved exclusively for evacuating 340,000 British soldiers across the English Channel. Refugees were not allowed to board, but Dad was dying. I had to get us on board.

"Although I was only 13, I was tall and looked older." She broke down crying. "I had to give up my virginity to get us smuggled on board in barracks bags. Dad died on the trip across the Channel. The soldiers did not want to be caught smuggling two civilians, so despite my protests, they buried him at sea."

Lucy was shaking so much she could not continue. Foster leaned over and hugged her. He extended his condolences. He poured more Bordeaux, and she laughed, "Now you see why I need fox terrier watch dogs — foxes keep the wolves away."

"Yes indeed," said Foster, "but not away from having another glass of wine." He skillfully changed the subject to the merits of Cabaret Sauvignon as compared to Merlot.

Later in the afternoon, he got a call from Groom, who was as excited as if he had just discovered a pot of Gold at the end of a rainbow. He had just come across an article about the death rate rising for middle class Americans. In the last decade, the death rate among whites aged 45 to 54, who had not been to College, had increased by over 20%. Why not admit more high school dropouts to Packard Village?

Foster was getting pretty fed up with ridiculous ideas from Groom. This one really took the cake. How many high school dropouts, or high school graduates if that mattered, could afford the initial fee? They would have to have won the lottery! But again he bit his tongue and said, "I'll cover that in my report."

Then Groom went on to a new concern. Some residents of Packard Village had lived so long that they had run out of enough money to pay the monthly fee. This shifted the shortage to the other residents. But suppose the other residents revolted and would not pay the increased burden?

This was news to Foster and seemed a genuine concern. Foster said he would look into it. He called his own lawyers, Tuthill and Townsand, in Stamford and they said, although they were not authorized to practice law in Florida, they could check it out and give him a "quick and dirty" answer which he could confirm, if he wished, with Florida counsel.

The next day, Thursday, Foster attended the 10 o'clock meeting of the Packard Investment Club. The members of the club sat at a rectangular table in the center of the room.

Guests, apparently wanting to join, crowded into seats along the walls. Foster took one of the last vacant seats.

A gentleman at the end of the table introduced himself as Fred Farley, the President. He welcomed the guests and explained this was a meeting of the investment committee that preceded the formal meeting. He turned the meeting over to Beverly Cole, the Investment Officer.

Beverly asked Ken Cornwell for news of Sanofi. Sanofi had not met its projected earnings in the last quarter and the stock was down. He did not have any news of successful clinical trials of the projected perpetual life drugs on which Sanofi held patents. But, according to *New Scientist* magazine, aging isn't irreversible; already the life of mice has been greatly elongated by drugs that prevent cells from becoming senescent. The trick is to find a way to cure the ends of RNA, which tend to fray as you age, so they no longer carry the correct message to replace worn out cells in your body. After extended discussion, the Investment Committee concluded it would continue to hold Sanofi despite its disappointing performance.

The president then called the meeting to order. A motion was made to increase the number of members, currently limited to twenty-five, to permit the many residents who were interested in perpetual life drugs to join. The pros and cons kicked off quite a ruckus and the President called the meeting into Executive Session and asked all the guests to leave.

When Foster told Groom he had been thrown out of the meeting, Groom became as excited as a fox breaking into a chicken coop. "If they have another meeting while you're there, raise hell about not letting in new members. Maybe it will give someone a heart attack!"

The next day he skipped his afternoon visit to the dog park in order to visit the Assisted Living Residence and get a report from Jean. He drove his rented golf cart east along the path on the southern boundary of the property. It passed lakes and ponds on his left and a slough on his right.

Both were an ornithologist's delight. On floats in the lakes, Anhinga were resting with their wings spread to dry in the afternoon sun. On the lakes several species of ducks paddled about. Along their shore great blue herons and lesser Louisiana green herons were waiting for a tasty fish to swim by.

In the swampy slough on his right he saw a giant egret marked by its long neck and yellow bill and quite a flock of smaller white birds. He would have to check them out in

Sibley's Bird Guide. *Were they cattle egrets or white ibis?* He asked a passing tram driver about the birds.

The driver said, "They are cattle egrets. I always come this way when it's not out of the way. I've even seen sand-hill and even whooping cranes in this slough." Just then a mother duck and her five ducklings waddled across the path, "Oh-oh", said the driver, "there used to be six little ones. The resident otter must have had little duck soup for supper."

Which one became Little Duck Soup?

When the ducks passed, Foster proceeded around two corners to the Assisted Living Residence. He was directed to

Jean's modest room and ample bathroom on the first floor. She was dressed in a becoming green and blue print dress and welcomed him warmly. He noticed a machine on the dresser next to her bed.

She said, "That is a nebulizer. I put on a mask and it helps me breathe."

She punched her talking clock and it said, "The time is four p.m. and the temperature is 78 degrees."

"Oh," she said, "it is Happy Hour. Let's see who is playing today."

She now used a walker to proceed down a hall to a large room. There were more than 20-odd residents scattered on couches and chairs listening to an accomplished pianist playing cocktail music. It reminded Foster of Bobby Short playing at the Carlisle in New York City. They were served scotch and sodas, and pigs in blankets as an appetizer. At five o'clock, the pianist wound up with "God Bless America" and they moved across the hall to a pleasant dining room. Its windows looked out on a pine forest.

A raccoon looked in; it appeared to be casing the joint. They were seated by the major domo at a table with three other ladies and a very deaf gentleman. They ordered from a menu that resembled the menu in the Chandelier Room.

Most of them ordered the seafood bisque soup. It was just the right temperature but one woman complained to the major domo that it was not hot enough. He graciously agreed that there was nothing worse than half hot soup and soon returned with a steaming bowl. Foster surmised that he must have a doctorate in reflexive/defensive psychology.

After dinner Foster had a long chat with Jean. She was laudatory about everything and everybody at Assisted Living, except the biddy that complained about the soup. A nurse came in to give her pills, then an aide came in to supervise her shower and Foster excused himself.

In the morning, he took stock of what he had found out in his first week. Being at Packard Village was a little like being at St. Knowitall Academy. There was too much to do and not enough time to do it. Also, they both fed you dinner. But there were two very big differences: First, here the food was very good. Second, if you failed to attend all the activities, say, the weekly forum or bible study, you did not have to go to detention.

He decided to get in a swim in the Gulf. Lucy had mentioned she loved to swim, so he called her up and asked her if she would like to join him. She thought it was a great idea. She had heard Lover's Key was only eight miles away and they might see manatees there. Foster had never seen a manatee, so he jumped at the idea. Lucy said she would be glad to take him in her Lexus.

When he joined her at her carport, she was clad in an attractive green beach coat. When they got to Lovers Key, she left her coat in the car and stepped out in a teeny-weeny green bikini that displayed a certain amount of cleavage as well as her elegant long legs and enticing curves as they attached to her body.

They rented a kayak. With Foster in the stern and Lucy in the bow they started paddling down the canals looking for manatees. They were startled by a tremendous splash when a tarpon leaped out of the water, but saw no manatees. Lucy complained that her long legs cramped up in the small kayak, so Foster nosed it ashore and helped her clamber out.

She said she could walk back to the rental area. So he turned around and paddled back towards it. As soon as he paddled around the first turn, he practically bumped into a pair of manatees. They didn't look like mermaids at all — sea cows was surely the more appropriate nickname.

When Foster reached the rental area, Lucy was already there. Her long legs had beat his most energetic paddling. They went to the beach for a swim. Foster's legs did not bother him swimming and they both enjoyed the waves and tepid water.

Later sunning on the beach, Foster slathered on some suntan lotion. He offered to apply some on Lucy but she said primly, "I'll do it myself, thank you."

They chatted about the Spanish being spoken by a nearby family. Lucy explained she was fluent in German and Dutch as well as Luxembourgese, and fairly fluent in French, but not in Spanish.

At meetings at the dog park the next week, he pieced together the rest of her story. She was bored to death by her priggish English cousins in Leeds, and teased by their young children, who called her Lux on account of her guttural accent in English or sometimes even LuLu. Nevertheless, she excelled in school and managed to get a scholarship to Columbia University in New York City. When she graduated she got a job as a secretary in an international company headquartered there.

She had worked for Richard Barksdale, who, as head of the company's European sales, found her language skills very useful. After Barksdale divorced his wife, he asked her to marry him. Although he was much older, she agreed. Then his company was merged into a larger conglomerate and he was forced out.

Luckily he had a golden parachute contract and they traveled for several years. Then he had a stroke and they moved to Packard Village. Shortly after the move, he died. Foster figured if she was 13 in 1940, and I was 10, here in 1999 she is only three years older than I am.

Foster remembered he had once read a letter from Benjamin Franklin recommending older women for seven reasons but only one came to mind. It was that once a woman has lost the luster of fresh beauty, she pays great attention to perfecting other ways to please men.

The next week Foster joined the weekly Friday festive hour at the Care Center. The room was crowded with patients, some in wheelchairs, more with walkers, and a few who relied on canes. Volunteer residents made up an orchestra, consisting of a pianist, a drummer, and two trumpeters.

They played old tunes such as "Chattanooga Choo-Choo" and "Roll Out the Barrel" passably well.

He asked one of the volunteers if many men participated. She said the men usually volunteered to be water boys, filling the patient's pitchers each morning. Obviously, the festive Fridays cheered the Care Center residents who were able to attend to live on to the next Friday.

Well, his two weeks were about up and he had at least a few inklings of why the residents exceeded their statistical life span. For one thing, there were 25 members of the Investment Club who had been told there were at least nine organisms that lived perpetually. They had invested in a drug company that held patents on a drug it believed could facilitate RNA replacing worn out cells with healthy new cells. Tests on mice had been successful; the drug increased their lifespan. Several internet sites, such as Healthier Talk, also claimed some organisms regenerated themselves for a perpetual life. He printed out the Healthier Talk report as follows:

> *Dear Reader, the tiny creature you see here should not exist. In fact, its very existence defies the most fundamental laws of nature.*

You see, instead of crumbling into a lifeless blob when old age, sickness or injury sets in, it regenerates itself and comes back to life stronger than it was before. Amazingly, it never dies.

Then there were the claims of the Perpetual Life Church. Foster stayed up late trying to figure out how to fashion his report. He finally went to bed after catching a nightly news report that a Category 4 or 5 hurricane named Delores was headed for central Florida, several hundred miles north of Packard Village.

Hurricane Dolores

Before 7 o'clock on Saturday morning, he was awakened by a rapid knocking on his door and a buzz on his doorbell. He dragged himself out of bed, and clad only in pajamas stumbled to open the door. It was Sally Halbertson, the building representative. She was no longer smiling. She reported Hurricane Delores had suddenly veered south and was destined to smack into Packard Village in a few hours. It was her duty to move all the people on the first floor to the second floor in case of flooding and to move all the people on the third floor to the second floor in case the roof blew off. She was hopeful he would move to the living room and welcome an elderly couple from the third floor to occupy the twin beds in his bedroom. Their names were Professor Mark and Corrine Weber.

A bit shocked, he asked, "Why did I not meet them at the building dinner?"

Sally answered, "They don't attend or mix with the other residents very often, but it will only be for a few days."

Within an hour the Professor and his wife arrived at, or rather blew in, his door, as by now the wind was howling. He hobbled in on a cane with a small bag of medicine and toiletries and she struggled in, pushing a walker loaded down with bags of canned foods, milk and juice.

He welcomed them and soon learned the Professor was from the Massachusetts Institute of Technology. Although a Harvard man himself, Foster could not help being impressed by having an M.I.T. professor and his wife as his "guests."

After chatting for a few minutes, Foster found the professor had specialized in understanding cognition in the human brain. He had determined that the brains of *Homo sapiens* had no more than three trillion cells, about the same as dolphins. He mentioned that elephants, whales and the extinct Neanderthals had bigger brains. But the new super computers had far more "cells" and worked faster. They would surely figure out how to replicate themselves, what with 3D printing and self-controlled vehicles.

Naturally, Foster discussed the means of prolonging human life and overpopulation with the professor. The professor thought it more than likely these computers would replace the human race before it overran planet Earth.

Just then their conversation was interrupted by a crash as the broken branch off a tree shattered one of the panels of glass lights next to the front door on the apartment's west side. Corrine and the professor retreated to the bedroom, while Foster struggled to block the water and wind now blowing east through the broken pane into the living room. Foster wondered, *Did God put a quietus on the professor's dire prophecy?*

Just then the wind stopped, the lights went out, and an almost eerie silence prevailed. Foster knew this was the eye of the storm. The next blow would come from the east and hit the vulnerable lanais and windows overlooking the lake. Putting the question of whether supercomputers had volition to the back of his mind, Foster dealt with the current reality that the storm would soon release its fury against the east windows. He managed to push the back of the couch against them. *Dog-gone it. Now it would be foolish to try to sleep on the couch next to the windows; I will have to doze in the recliner.*

Sure enough, not long after he had the couch braced against the east windows, the wind and wind-blown debris crashed into the east side of the building and kept it up most of the day. By nightfall, Delores had moved across Florida to the Atlantic Ocean.

Foster and his guests broke bread together for the first meal of the day. They were still without electricity or any means of heat. Besides bread, Foster had a bag of apples and milk that would soon spoil in his refrigerator as it warmed to room temperature. Corrine contributed a can of sliced pineapple she had brought with her.

The building representative came by before dark with good news and bad news. The good news was that several residents had gas camp stoves and by the next morning would set up a kitchen in the second floor hall with prom-ises of at least hot coffee. The bad news was that the east windows in the Webster's third floor apartment had blown in and it was a sodden mess. The Webster's were not up to inspecting the damage and spent another night in Foster's bedroom, while he struggled to sleep on the recliner.

All the Building One residents were in good spirits at the communal breakfast in the second floor hall the next morning. Lucy Barksdale arrived at Foster's damp apartment pushing a shopping cart full of groceries. She said, "I knew you had just arrived here and probably did not have time to stock hurricane supplies."

Foster thought, *Here is a caring soul, a woman with more than pretty legs and a skimpy bikini.* Foster gave her another hug.

She was cordially greeted by Corrine Webster. They had taken art classes together. She also had a camp stove and they had a splendid lunch of hot split pea soup and ham and Swiss cheese sandwiches.

Afterward, the professor, aided by Foster, dragged himself up the flight of stairs to the third floor to inspect the damage to his spacious apartment. It truly was a soggy mess. The big window facing the lake was broken and rain had blown across the living room and on into the master bedroom through its open door. The kitchen and bathrooms were the only rooms that were usable. Foster would have to house the brain professor and his wife for at least another night.

Part of the Packard staff had been trapped in the Care Center and Assisted Living Residence by the hurricane. By the next morning, most of the Packard staff had made their way back to work over the washed out roads and around downed trees. Soon boxed lunches were distributed and it was announced that dinner would be served from a limited menu.

When telephone service was restored, Foster received a call from Groom. After saying hello, he said, "The news has reported hurricane Delores has crossed over southern Florida. Was Packard Village hit and were there any casualties?"

"We were hit hard, but there were no casualties to my knowledge," said Foster, "but I'll check with the Care Center and Assisted Living." He went to both and made inquiries.

He called Groom back. He reported that the Wellness Clinic was overwhelmed with treating bumps and bruises and that a 101-year-old woman had died in the night following the hurricane.

Groom was delighted. He chortled, "One less mouth to feed, and maybe one less aide to employ." After that he asked, "Was the hurricane the cause?"

Foster said, "Packard Village does not give out the cause of death, but I learned from another patient that she had been on oxygen for congestive heart failure. Without electricity, her nebulizer did not work. At her age when she came to Packard Village, she was expected to live nine years, but she actually lived 19 years."

Groom said, "What a damn shame."

This remark cold be taken as condolence or glee. Foster suspected the latter meaning. The more Foster heard from Groom, the less he liked him.

In the next few days, Foster pitched in with the residents and staff in cleaning up the debris and drying up the apartments. He was concerned with mold.

He asked Ken Cornwell about mold. Ken told him "There are an estimated 400,000 types of mold. Of these about 150,000 types have been identified by microscope and named. About 150 types are known to be dangerous to human health, particularly a black mold, Stachbetrys and a black and yellow mold, Aspergillus. On the other hand there are at least 15 types of benign mold, some of which flavor hard cheeses, such as Roquefort, Gorgonzola, and Stilton, or the outside of soft cheeses such as Brie and Camembert."

Ken went on, "After you run your air conditioner for a few days, buy some white bread in a bakery or baked in a grocery store. Be sure not to get commercial loaves, loaded with long shelf life chemicals. Put a slice of this fresh white on several butter plates around your apartment. If they mold within a week, move out and have the apartment professionally dehumidified. If they mold after two weeks look for or get the apartment inspected for a possible leak. If they don't mold in three weeks, the bread will be stale and ideal for making croutons for a delectable Caesar Salad."

It took a few days more for the professor's apartment to dry out. Finally, Foster helped his involuntary guests to move back upstairs. The professor and his wife both thanked him, and the professor insisted on giving him a book titled *String Theory for Dummies.* Later when Foster tried to understand the book, he found the title to be a complete oxymoron; the string theory is not for dummies, it is for super geeks in mathematics and physics.

With the couple gone, he tried to move the heavy couch he had pushed against the east windows back to its original position. In doing so, he severely wrenched his back. He went to the Wellness Clinic to have it treated. He was X-rayed, expertly strapped up and spent the night in the Care Center to await the report of the radiologist.

His semi-private room had two beds, reclining chairs, bureau, small closet and a bath. He was fortunate not to have a roommate and was placed in the bed by the window. It had an excellent view of the parking lot of an adjacent building.

The nurses and their aides were most helpful. He was served an excellent dinner in the second floor dining room gladdened with a glass of red wine. In the morning the pleasant head nurse, Tricia, said, "I have some good news and bad news. The good news is the Radiologist says the X-rays reveal no break, dislocation or disc trouble with your spine. The Doctor says take it easy for a week and your back muscles should be fine. The bad news is that the Collier County Health Department has locked down Packard Village in quarantine. Several of our patients have contracted a dangerous virus, the Trinotic Flu. I don't know how long the quarantine will last."

Foster had his cell phone with him and immediately called Groom and explained he did not want to bring the Trinotic Flu north. Groom was happy as a clam at high tide to hear that the Trinotic Flu spread easily and could be fatal. Nevertheless, he said Guzman was bugging him for the report. Foster pointed out that he did not have his laptop with him and could not prepare a written report until he was back in his apartment.

At least mail was delivered to the Care Center during the Quarantine. Foster received a lively, loving and caring note from Lucy Barksdale every day. She said Rolex and Timex watch out for you. He also received a letter from Tuthill and Townsman. In their opinion any shortfall in payments of the monthly fee charged by Packard Village to a resident had to be made up by the entity that had received the entrance fee, the Packard Holding Company.

He also chatted at lunch and dinner in the dining room with the other Care Center occupants. One elderly gentleman, Scotty, discussed the rise of the Muslim religion and the fact that the birth rate of Christians in England and Sweden was less than two children per couple and that of Muslims was over four. He pointed out that in a few generations these countries would have a Muslim majority. The mayor of London was already a Muslim.

Finally, Foster asked, "Well, sir, Muslims strongly believe in the hereafter, do you also believe in the hereafter?"

Scotty scratched his head and replied "Why yes, I do, every time I go into a new room or open a closet door, I say *'What in the world am I here after?'*"

Many of the patients in the Care Center were forgetful, but as time dragged on he met a woman, Mary by name, who was a real chatterbox. She told him the next step up the ladder to heaven was Avow Hospice. She said she had visited friends there. "It is a truly beautiful place. Each room is private with a bath. The rooms have polished oak floors. They also have a private screened in porch overlooking a small lake. Along the lake there are many beautiful benches dedicated to departed loved ones. And it does not cost anything, Medicare pays."

When Foster mentioned this in his daily telcon with Groom, Groom was delighted. "Get the Administration there to extol the advantages for the residents to move on to a Hospice and avoid costly, life-threatening operations. Get them to read *Being Mortal* by Dr. Atul Gewande. It is a great book."

For once Groom had said something worth considering. Foster had also received a letter from Buddy Allen. With Foster gone so long, Buddy opened a discussion with a rival actuarial firm in Hartford. Would Foster consider being bought out? Foster called Buddy to learn the name of the principal of the Hartford firm. He learned it was none other than Anson Chadwick, a very genial fellow he had met at a Harvard reunion. It was certainly worth considering. Florida and Packard Village provided two of his loves, fishing and contract bridge, and maybe also Lucy.

Then Groom called back again. Guzman had been checking on the possibility of perpetual life with other members of his staff. Much to Groom's chagrin and Guzman's dismay, they had been told that a scarlet jellyfish with the scientific name of Astaxanthin had been discovered by Italian scientists in 1996. It could regenerate itself and live forever! If Groom checked this out and it proved to be true, Guzman was going to divest himself of Packard Village.

Foster again Googled Healthier Talk and found they had changed the picture of the jellyfish. They now claimed it looked like this:

Foster concluded that Healthier Talk should be renamed Double Talk, about as reliable as the candidates running for President of the United States.

CHAPTER FIVE

The Trinotic Flu

In the Care Center, Foster soon got bored with daytime television and wandered down to the reading room at the end of the hall where he was told he could find books to read. He had been too young to serve in World War II, but had been fascinated to read about it.

He found the Care Center's Library consisted of a large bureau with three drawers full of large print books. In the second drawer he found Rick Atkinson's *An Army at Dawn,* a history of our early landing at Dakar in Africa and the subsequent North African campaign.

After getting our troops safely ashore, he turned out the lights and went to sleep. About two in the morning he woke up. His teeth were chattering uncontrollably. He pressed the emergency button and Nancy, the night nurse, appeared in a few seconds.

She checked his blood pressure and temperature, then shown a light on his tongue. "Oh-oh," she said, "You're down with the second case of Trinotic Flu on this floor. I see you are reading *An Army at Dawn*. I'm afraid you'll have time to read the rest of Rick Atkinson's trilogy, *The Day of Battle* and *Guns at Last Light*, before you leave here.

Foster was miserable. He spent most of the first week going at both ends. He was better the second week and his back was fine! He was able to dine with the other ambulatory residents in the dining room. Several of them were capable of intelligent conversation.

One lady, in particular, recovering from a bout with pneumonia, was one of the founders of the Packard Village Foundation. It was dedicated to help defray the cost of education for aspiring employees, their children, and other eleemosynary endeavors. It had received approval as a tax-exempt charitable organization from the Internal Revenue Service. She obviously hoped Foster could make a contribution. He mentioned the Foundation in one of his telephone conferences with Groom.

At the end of the third week, since his was the last case of the flu at Packard Village, the quarantine was lifted. Unfortunately, it was time to fish or cut bait with the darned report. Suppose he just said to Mr. Guzman: Packard Village is adorned with a beautiful variety of flowering trees, bushes, shrubs and its grounds are laced by many different colorful flowers. It provides habitats for otters, raccoons, rabbits, squirrels, feral cats and occasionally panthers. Its' trees, sloughs and skies are adorned by a wide variety of birds, of many shapes and vibrant colors. Its lakes provide habitat for ducks and other waterfowl. In addition, its lakes have a variety of fish and are visited regularly by otters and rarely by an alligator.

He would add the staff at Packard Village is friendly, courteous and efficient at providing the residents with nutritious and delicious meals and a wide variety of activities that challenges their minds and physiques. He would note the residents had established a tax-exempt foundation to provide funds for scholarships for members of the staff and their children and other eleemosynary endeavors. In addition, to enrich the souls of the residents, there are a plethora of religious services held at or conveniently near the Village. Furthermore, the residents are generally happy and many believe they will live until perpetual life, which many believe to be just around the corner, arrives.

Then, he would ask Buddy Allen to polish this up and attach at least thirty pages of the boiler plate statistics he had prepared for the State of Connecticut in connection with a recent study of the cost of its pension plans. Buddy and Penny would have to be absolutely certain that they changed all the headings from State of Connecticut to Pack-ard Village, and Buddy would have to insert a table showing how much the lifespan of the residents of the Village exceeded the norm.

Finally the report would recommend that a further detailed study of the residents be made. It would compare the life span of residents using supplements prepared from the perpetual jellyfish to the life span of residents that did not use it. He would ask for an additional fee of $10,000 to conduct such a study.

1937 Packard Rumble Seat Coupe

CHAPTER SIX

The Everglades

When he returned to his apartment, even though Packard Village encompassed almost 200 acres, Foster was feeling a little shut in. When Ken Cornwall asked him if he would like to split the cost of a fishing charter, he jumped at the chance.

He called Lucy and asked her to meet him at the dog park. He asked if she wished to fish, but she said she would prefer another trip to Lover's Key. She said she had tried to learn to hit a golf ball while he had been quarantined. She was most surprised the golf pro was a woman. Lucy said she had to laugh at her lesson at a short hole.

After many practice swings Lucy described how her first shot had sailed over the green and into the lake beyond. The woman pro told her to choke up the club two inches. The next shot landed in long rough grass before the hole. Lucy said from now on walking Timex and Rolex and swimming were plenty of exercise. They made a date for another trip to Lovers Key that next week.

Foster was delighted he had found a fishing companion at Packard Village. His dad had taught him to cast a fly rod on the back lawn in Greenwich. Then for his first fishing trip, his dad had taken him to fish the Ausable River in the Adirondack Mountains of New York State. He had trouble navigating the stream, which seemed to be lined with stones as slippery as greased cannon balls. His dad then splurged on a pair of wading shoes with hobnail heels and felt soles.

So outfitted, he was able to wade the stream and using a Royal Coachman fly landed several lunch-sized brown trout. Thus, on this first outing, like the fish, he had been hooked on fishing.

Ken said fishing in the 10,000 islands was the closest you could come to fishing northern free stone streams in the Adirondacks, Catskills or Poconos. He explained the best place to get away from civilization was to fish the backwater out of Everglades City. He knew a Captain named Snapper Bishop down there. They made a reservation for the next Saturday.

That day Ken drove him down southeast about 40 miles along the Tamiami Trail. Along the way, they crossed the Fakahatchee Strand. He explained it divided the water flow from southwest and southeast Florida and was famous for the rare ghost orchid, bald cypress trees and an unusual spikey grass, called fakahatchee or gamma grass. He commented that Everglades City was once the County Seat of Collier County, but now was better known for Square Grouper than black grouper.

Foster asked, "What in the world is Square Grouper?"

"They are tightly bound bales of marijuana gently parachuted from the sky by aeroplanes from Columbia or Central America," replied Ken. "Once I heard every man in Everglades City was arrested for being in the Square Grouper trade, but I don't know how the suit turned out."

They turned right on a side road south five miles to Everglades City and parked next to a long rambling white Inn called The Rod & Gun Club, lying along the Barron River. President Howard Taft was said to have stayed there, but lacking sprinklers, it now only housed a restaurant.

They had reserved a cabin adjacent to the Inn. The Inn was located next to a dock along the Barron River. Several snappy looking white fishing boats were berthed along the dock. From one of them Captain Snapper Butler called "Hi, Ken."

Ken introduced Captain Butler to Foster. "Mr. Foster, meet Captain Snapper Butler, the Mayor of Everglades City and our guide for the day."

Foster said, "Good to meet you, my first name is George."

The boat was neat as a pin, with dual outboard motors. There were six spinning rods in a rack and a saltwater bait bin loaded with live shrimp in the stern.

Cruising down the Barron River, they soon left the last marker buoy behind and entered 10,000 islands covered by mangroves all looking alike. They passed only one other fishing boat. Its Captain cried, "We've got pompano!"

Soon they were completely alone. "We're now here where few men of any color, red, white, black or yellow, have ever been," said Captain Bishop. He then added, "Quick, look up," pointing to the cloudless sky. Hundreds of feet above them a bald eagle was swooping down on an osprey clutching a fish. The osprey soon dropped the fish and the robber eagle soared down to retrieve his ill-gotten gain.

After this rarely observed event, they nosed in close to the mangroves overhanging a small island and carefully cast just short of the end of the overhang. Soon they began to catch good-sized red fish, some more than 24 inches long. They kept enough for their dinner and also caught several pompano on the way home.

They fileted their catch at the dock and arranged to have the red fish cooked at The Rod & Gun Club that evening. They were about as sweet a fish as Foster had ever tasted.

Over several glasses of Chardonnay at dinner Ken and Foster segued into a discussion of the miracle of life, its great adventures and misadventures. Foster had been raised as a Presbyterian but had attended church mostly for weddings or funerals.

Ken said everyone has faith. Even atheists have faith that they exist, and most atheists believe the Universe also exists.

He understood the need of some people to be governed by a highly disciplined set of beliefs, such as the Muslims, Lutherans and Catholics. Of course, not all those professing adherence to disciplined religions did as they were bidden. Some Muslims drank alcohol.

He mentioned that on a guided trip to Italy, the garrulous guide lady had remarked that 95% of Italians were Catholics but only 5% practiced Catholicism. He noted mankind had a universal craving to explain how matter, energy and life, good or evil, came into existence. He admitted his smattering of ignorance of the many eastern religions seeking to answer these questions.

He said he was a Unitarian Universalist because for one thing, it freed him from the possible misuse of power, by those, such as the Spanish Inquisition or Muslim extremists, claiming to enforce the will of their, the only, God. It empowered him to select the best of many beliefs and enjoy the beauty and diversity of his brief trip on spaceship Earth, which he did not expect to become perpetual in his lifetime. He said the UUs sponsored many beneficial causes.

Foster mulled over Ken's views as he sipped a demitasse of coffee after dinner and said he might attend a UU service the next Sunday. Maybe Lucy would like to join him.

They spent the night in their Cabin. The next morning they threw their bags in the trunk and started to motor back to Packard Village, but soon Ken slammed on the brakes and went back to the Cabin to get his broad brimmed hat. "You know," he said, "I'm always leaving it behind when I wear it to dinner at the Village. That is because there is not a single hat rack in the Village and you have to put your hat under your seat or in the nearest closet, if any. Packard Village must be in cahoots with the American Association of Dermatology. Due to the lack of hat racks, almost no one wears a hat. If you can judge from the number of residents who have a band aids on their nose, face ears or scalp, almost everyone gets a squamous or basal cell carcinoma and sometimes a deadly pernicious melanoma caused by the rays of the pitiless Florida sun."

He added Packard Village ought to heed the threat of the Irish singer at Bill's Gay Nineties in New York who sang, "I had a hat when I came in, and put it right there on the rack, and I'll have a hat when I go out, or I'll break somebody's back." He had previously mentioned the lack of hat racks to Groom, who told him never to mention the need for hat racks to the management of Packard Village. Instead extol the benefits of plenty of sunshine, which helps the body produce Vitamins.

When they returned to Packard Village, he opened his mailbox. He found it crammed full with a draft of his Packard Village Report and a proposed contract for the sale of his business. He knew Penny must have been careful when she typed it because the word Connecticut never appeared. He faxed a few minor changes to her and to protect against any possibility of a successful lawsuit added a ten-point caveat as follows:

The estimated life spans of the residents of Packard Village set forth in this report does not take into account:

1. The increase in life spans due to the use of 3D (three -dimensional) printers to print replacement human glands hearts, livers, lungs, pancreases and other organs that will not trigger an attack by the recipient's immune system. Also the increase in life span when the DNA of pigs is altered so that their organs will not be rejected a when transplanted in humans.

2. The increase in life spans due to the excellent hospitals, clinics and doctors in south west Florida.

3. The possibility that Packard Village will install convenient hat racks and decrease deaths due to pernicious melanoma and other skin cancers.

4. The possibility that Big Sisters of America will establish a branch in Packard Village to provide a sister for residents who are an only child or whose sisters have died.

5. The possibility that the American Croquet Association will substitute "unalive" for "dead" to describe a ball that has hit another ball without first becoming alive by going through another wicket.

6. The increase in life spans by living in a caring community with a helpful and optimistic staff that encourages many festivities.

7. The increase in life spans by eating extracts from purple jellyfish that live forever.

8. The increase in life spans by believing in perpetual life and refusing to believe that computers will acquire volition to rule the World.

9. The increase in life spans from the availability of locally grown fresh fruit and vegetables, such as avocadoes, beans, mangoes, oranges, strawberries and

tomatoes and locally caught fish, such as grouper, pompano, snapper and red fish.

10. The increase in life span by excluding male College Graduates.

He asked Buddy to clear the caveats with Tuthill and Townsman and send the report on to Guzman. He also asked Buddy to have that firm to get in touch with Anson Chadwick's lawyers, Mark & Sudarsky, in Hartford and finalize the proposed contact for sale of his business now that he had decided to make Packard Village his home.

CHAPTER SEVEN

The Twentieth Anniversary

It was the year 2010 and Packard Village was preparing to celebrate its 20th Anniversary on the Fourth of July. Traditionally the Fourth was celebrated with a parade of golf carts, which most of the residents decorated with American Flags and red, white and blue bunting.

Packard's founder, Dr. Noah Packard himself, had returned recently as a resident. He was still hale and hearty in his eighties and, at the urging of the Lifestyle Director, he had agreed to drive his 1937 Packard Rumble Seat Coupe at the head of the Anniversary Parade. It would wind slowly through the Village on the sinuous golf course paths followed by hundreds of golf carts. Barrier stakes to bar vehicles other than golf carts had been removed to permit the Packard to lead the Parade.

One of the residents, a former owner of a steel mill in Birmingham, Alabama, said he was going to decorate his Cart with four Confederate flags, crossed bars with stars for the seven states of the Confederacy on a red background. When news of this plan reached the Executive Director, he was told that he was free to display them, but could not participate in the parade. Packard Village relied on many African-American employees and had a program to help those born in foreign lands to become citizens of the United States.

Abagail, the attractive and enthusiastic Lifestyle Director, distributed lottery tickets to all the ladies who wished to participate as the Queen of the Parade. The winner would ride in the rumble seat and throw baubles to onlookers. Lucy drew ticket seventeen which proved to be the winning ticket.

Foster called Groom to see if he or Mr. Guzman would like to participate in the festivities. No, Mr. Guzman was engaged in a major transaction and had no time to spare visiting Packard Village. Then Groom went into his usual rant about the paucity of deaths at Packard Village, even with the deadly Trinotic flu there.

He had a new scheme to bar the admission of potentially long-lived applicants. No person should be admitted if he or she had sisters. He said all you have to do is to Goggle siblings on the internet to find that having living sisters increases longevity. This was not news to Foster; he had already alluded to the beneficial effect of sisters in his caveats. He had read many books on the subject of how siblings affected each other.

The next day, Foster was invited to play croquet at 9 o'clock in the morning. He had purchased and was decked out to play in, a white hat, shirt, shorts, sox and sneakers.

No sooner had he arrived to play, than the attractive young lady who was the assistant to the Executive Director found him on the Court. She said, "Thank goodness I found you. Don't you have a cell phone? I checked your room, the gym, the swimming pools and here you are. A Mr. Groom called, and while I told him it is not our practice to search for residents who do not answer their telephone calls, he said this was a life and death matter."

Foster had not yet received his fee, so he reluctantly told the other players he had to take the call and returned to his room to call Groom back.

Groom was practically breathless when he answered. "Guzman has just closed the Transatlantic deal, the transaction I mentioned, at a great profit. There were at least a score of attorneys, accountants, and agents of the title companies at the closing. After receiving your report, he has decided to donate his interest in Packard Village to the tax exempt Packard Village Foundation."

Oh-oh, thought Foster, *here it goes again.*

Groom went on, "Keep this news confidential, deep six your report, and don't let any retrievable copies continue to exist in your computer; he plans to deduct the original purchase price from his tax returns, not a price based on your longevity projections"

"Well," said Foster, "good luck with the IRS, but I'm not sure the Foundation is up to running a CCRC. Let me tell the generous ladies that founded it about their good fortune or possible headaches."

"You keep out of that!" said Groom. "Mr. Guzman wants to publicize his generosity by attending the 20th Anniversary, Fourth of July celebration. He'll announce it at that time."

"Okay," said Foster. "Dr. Packard, the founder of the Village, is going to head the Golf Cart parade in his 1937 Packard Coupe. The Queen of the Parade will be riding in the rumble seat – maybe Mr. Guzman would like to ride with her as King."

"What an idea," said Groom. "I'll ask him."

A few weeks later, on July 3rd, Mr. Guzman arrived at Packard Village. He was greeted by Thomas Fletcher, the *Interim* Executive Director, and escorted to the best suite in the Guest Lodge. He explained that he would like to make a brief announcement effecting the future of Packard Village at the conclusion of the parade. He asked Fletcher to have the parade wind up in the principal parking lot and arrange for loudspeakers so that all could hear the news.

After Fletcher left, he called Foster. "George," he said, "join me at the English Pub for a drink before dinner."

When they met, Foster noticed that Guzman had put on even more weight. They both ordered single malt scotches on the rocks. Guzman said, "My favorite is Isle of Skye, but it is hard to find."

Foster admitted he had never heard of it, then inquired, "How is Aaron Groom doing?"

"Huh?" said Guzman. "I imagine he is standing in line at the local office of the Department of Labor begging for unemployment compensation. You know what that damn fool told me?" asked Guzman, lighting a Marlboro cigarette.

"Groom claimed I could make money on Packard Village if I limited applicants to male High School or even College drop outs, who did not have sisters, living or dead, who did not eat extracts from purple jellyfish, who drank and smoked heavily, who did not believe in perpetual life and so on and so on. When you add that to the fact that you really need a portfolio of at least a million dollars to afford one of our larger apartments, probably the only person in the United States who fits that description is me! Come to think of it, he is still on the Board of Directors of Packard Holding Company. I'll have to hold a meeting to correct that."

Foster was nonplussed. Finally, he said, "I will be glad to work with you directly or whoever you delegate to oversee Packard Village."

"When Groom told me he had spilled the beans to you that I planned to donate my stock in the Packard Holding Company to the Packard Village Foundation, that was the last straw," replied Guzman. "At least he said he told you to keep it quiet."

"Yup," said Foster. "Not even a mouse, or here in Packard Village, except for me, not even a newt or salamander or ghost ant, knows."

The Fourth turned out to be an overcast morning. By nine o'clock, more than 100 golf carts, some decorated to a fare-the-well with American flags, red, white and blue bunting, balloons, and even whirling propellers, were assembled in line behind Dr. Packard in his 1937 Packard rumble seat coupe. Lucy was already in the rumble seat, her head adorned with a realistic crown made of paper.

Then, to the clarion call of a bugle, Guzman, accompanied by Thomas Fletcher, appeared. He was introduced as the owner of the Village's parent company and crowned by Fletcher as King of the parade. Some residents in the golf carts remembered the abdication of King Farouk of Egypt in 1952. They immediately dubbed Guzman "Farouk the Fat."

Fletcher had a sturdy step stool to help the King climb into the rumble seat with Lucy. Lucy, who already had difficulty bending her long legs to fit in the rumble seat, found it doubly difficult entwined with the legs of such a rotund King.

In the few minutes they waited for the last tardy carts to get in line, Guzman introduced himself to Lucy. He told her this was a great day for him and an even greater day for

Packard Village. He was going to announce a great gift to its residents at the end of the parade.

Finally with the last cart in line, Fletcher jumped into the front seat with Dr. Packard to guide him on the narrow golf cart paths. After winding past the Assisted Living Residence, Care Center and East Club House, the parade slowed briefly as a free cup of coffee was passed into the carts. Fletcher signaled for everyone to move on because of the lowering skies.

Just as they entered a narrow part of the cart path along an arm of Sunset Lake, Fletcher saw a flash of lightning. Fletcher was well aware that Florida's heat and humidity begets about 35,000 lightning strikes a year, 5 to 20 of them fatal to humans. He waited for a second flash and counted less than two seconds before he heard thunder. It was too close for comfort — less than 8 miles away.

Fletcher immediately asked Dr. Packard to stop his Packard. He jumped out and trotted back along the line of carts, calling for their drivers to take cover. This was hardly necessary for those of them not too deaf to hear thunder. They were already pulling out of line, some to go forward towards their buildings in front of the line and others to go back to their buildings lying to the rear.

This resulted in a bit of a melee around the Packard coupe. It was situated on the narrowest part of the path, half way between the lake and a construction fence. To let the carts pass, Dr. Packard shifted into reverse and attempted to back off the path. He had trouble turning the polished wooden steering wheel of his pride and joy – which long predated power steering and power brakes. He gave the steering wheel a great heave and his right foot hit the accelerator spinning the coupe halfway into the lake.

The King and Queen in the rumble seat were up to their necks in water. Lucy's long legs stood her in good stead as she scrambled out of the rumble seat. She was standing waist deep with her feet stuck in the muddy lake bottom. She saw that Guzman was struggling to get out of the rumble seat so she reached out with her right arm to help him. In doing so, she slipped in the muck and gashed her outstretched arm on the metal corner of the open rumble seat. Her crown fell off her head and forlornly, it floated away.

Foster, whose cart was near the head of the parade, ran to help pull her up the bank. She collapsed on the bank, holding her long skirt to staunch the flow of blood from the gash in her arm. Foster then saw Guzman still struggling to get out of the rumble seat. With the help of Thomas

Fletcher, Ken Cornwall and others they pulled Guzman out of the rumble seat and buoyed him to shore. He lay prostrate on the bank.

Although really more concerned with the condition of his automobile, hovering on the bank of Sunset Lake with its rumble seat in the drink, Dr. Packard felt Guzman's pulse, tapped his chest and said, "This man has had a heart attack or a stroke."

Fletcher pulled out his cell phone and called for an ambulance.

In less than 10 minutes, an ambulance and fire truck arrived at the closest road to the site of the accident. Two hearty paramedics rolled a gurney to the edge of the Lake. As he was being lifted on the gurney, Guzman motioned to Foster. "George, take the papers out of my hip pocket," he muttered.

Foster managed to pull out a wet sheaf of papers, tearing them in the process. Then the paramedics put an oxygen mask on Guzman and rolled him away. Foster turned to the drenched and bedraggled Lucy, her striking white Queen's gown now splattered with both mud and blood. Foster said, "You better go along in the ambulance, too, and have a doctor look at that arm."

"No thanks," said Lucy. "It is just a bad scratch; take me to the Wellness Clinic and then to my apartment for some dry clothes." On the way to the Wellness Clinic, she said, "I'll bet those papers are the speech Guzman was going to make. He said he going to make a really great gift to the Packard Village Foundation."

After the nurses at the Wellness Clinic had cleaned, sanitized and bound up Lucy's wounded arm so tightly it hurt, Foster took her back to her apartment and arranged for the Fourth's picnic lunch to be delivered. He then carried the wet papers back to his apartment and called his lawyers in Stamford, Tuthill and Townsman, for information on how to deal with wet papers. Not unexpectedly, they were closed for the Fourth. So as a last resort he checked the Internet.

CHAPTER EIGHT

The Wet Paper Fracas

Foster found specific instructions for wet paper treatment on the internet. Following these instructions, he washed off the green slime from the first page, straightened out the torn last page as best he could, and then placed aluminum foil between each page and laid them carefully on an empty shelf in his refrigerator's freezer.

Before reviewing the papers the next morning, Foster called Lucy to see how she felt. She said her arm throbbed and she had made an appointment with a doctor in the afternoon. Foster offered to take her to the doctor and she gladly accepted. Then she said, "Did you hear what happened to Mr. Guzman at the emergency room? The doctors found it was a stroke and he is paralyzed."

"Good Lord," said Foster. "What am I supposed to do with the papers he handed me?" As soon as he hung up, he lifted the first sheet out of the refrigerator. Some of the ink had washed away with the slime, but it was possible to make out that Guzman knew that John Adams had predicted that the signing of the Declaration of Independence would be celebrated. As near as he could make out, Guzman had planned to say:

> *'It is a great day for the United States of America and Packard Village, its residents and staff. I was most honored to ride in your parade in a vintage Packard, lovingly restored by your founder, Dr. Noah Packard. You know John Adams predicted the signing of the Declaration of Independence would be long celebrated, although he got the date wrong.' This is what John Adams said.*

At this point the creases made it impossible to read the rest of the first page, so Foster looked up the Adams' quote. It went: "The second day of July, 1776, will be the most memorable Epocha in the History of America. I am apt to believe that it will be celebrated, by succeeding generations, as the great anniversary Festival. It ought to be solemnized as the day of Deliverance by Acts of Devotion to

God Almighty. It ought to be solemnized with Pomp and Parade, with Shows, Games, Sports, Guns, Bells, Bonfires and Illuminations from one end of this Continent to the other from this time forward forever more."

Turning to the second sheet, only the first paragraph was legible, Guzman went on,

> *I also want to thank Mr. Fletcher and the entire staff of Packard Village, who have prepared a sumptuous Fourth of July Picnic Lunch, which I am sure you are anxious to sample soon. However, before you go, I have an announcement to make to the residents of Packard Village. I plan to give all the capital stock of the Packard Holding Company to the Packard Village Foundation. The Foundation will thereafter have the power to control the management of Packard Village in accordance with the provisions of Law, and I hope will do so for the benefit of both the residents and staff.*

The rest of the page and the next two pages were only partially legible.

Foster was in a quandary about what to do with these papers. He again called his Stamford lawyers and reached Stoddard Townsman. Townsman grilled him on his connection with Guzman. He summed it up as follows, "Well, you have never been an employee of Mr. Guzman or his corporation, your principal connection has been as a professional consultant to prepare a report, which you completed and delivered. I believe you should treat those papers the same way you would treat a diamond ring he handed you before being put in an ambulance. You are not a bailee for hire but a gratuitous bailee and so have only ordinary duty of care. You should return them to him at his request."

"But he has had a paralyzing stroke," Foster interjected.

"Then, hold them for his guardian," said Townsman.

Foster thought about this. If he had been hired to hold a diamond ring, he should have put it in a safe deposit box, but as a gratuitous holder he might have felt safe by hiding it in the ice box, even though he had heard burglars often checked there. Well, they checked for jewelry but probably not for frozen notes for a speech, so he put the four sheets back in the freezer.

Foster did not know who Guzman's guardian might be so he called Barbara Baxter, Guzman's secretary in New York

City. She was most distraught to hear of the stroke and when asked about the guardian, said, "Oh dear, Samuel Wallace, an old friend, is still his guardian and Vice Chairman of the Board of the Packard Holding Company, but Mr. Guzman was considering a change. Confidentially, since Mr. Wallace retired as Chairman of a Worldwide News Service, he has become increasingly addicted to a particular brand of Tennessee whiskey, and is rarely sober."

"Oh-oh," said Foster. "Probably a fan of Jack Daniels, at least he picked a good brand, but I'll still need his telephone number and address."

"Why don't you call Aaron Groom instead, he is still on the Board and he knows all about the retirement communities. I'll give you his number and address, too."

"Believe me, he has my number and I sure enough have his number," said Foster, "but do give me his address." By the time he had the telephone numbers and addresses, it was time for lunch.

Foster picked up Lucy for the doctor's visit and they grabbed well stuffed tacos and iced tea at a Mexican lunch spot on the way. She was patched up with three stitches and received a tetanus shot and anti-biotic prescription. Before filling the prescription, Foster took her back to her apartment for a nap.

Instead of lying down and listening to soft music, she insisted on talking about her conversation with Guzman in the rumble seat. "He talked quite a bit," she said, "about the gift he was making to the Packard Village Foundation. I thought the Foundation was primarily for the education of employees, and I told him so. I had discussed it with Corrine Webster in Art Class. I believe she was one of its founders."

Actuaries like lawyers try to pin things down, so Foster said, "Did Guzman say 'I *have made* a gift' or 'I *plan* to make or *am going to make* a gift?'"

Lucy was not sure.

The next morning , Foster decided that making a call to Samuel Wallace should be the first order of business. He waited until ten o'clock in the morning to make the call, hoping Wallace was up and sober by that time. He was delighted; he found Wallace sober as a judge. Wallace said he had already heard the sad news from Barbara Baxter and had sent flowers to Guzman in the Hospital.

Then Foster told him he was holding four pages of the speech Guzman planned to make in his freezer. Wallace said he'd dealt with illegible and damaged papers throughout his career and to call ERC Services and follow their advice. He then told Wallace about Guzman's plan to give the stock of the holding company to a charitable foundation and bury his report.

"Well," said Wallace, "as his guardian, I am entitled to know the basis for Mr. Guzman's speech."

"In a nutshell," Foster replied, "as an actuary I found the residents of Packard Village were living three years, four months and two days longer than normal for their age group on admittance to Packard Village."

"Wow," said Wallace. "When Peter Pickering was nominated to be Secretary of the Treasury, he decided a blind trust should divest itself from any investments that require continuing attention. He called me to help the Trustee find a buyer for his CRCCs and put me in touch with his assistant, Robert Benny. Benny supplied most of the information about the CCRCs. Give him a call."

Foster did so and, after filling Benny in about the speech notes and stroke, questioned him about any warranties made in the sale. Benny said no warranties had been given about the expected death rate, but it was common knowledge that the medical profession and drug companies were making life-extending advances all the time.

Foster told him that residents of Packard Village were living more than three years longer than expected. Benny pointed out that most people would pay a pretty penny for three extra years of life. As soon as Foster reported this to Wallace, Wallace called Gerald Guzman, who already planned to go to Florida.

By the next day, Samuel Wallace and Gerald Guzman were both at Grandpa's side in a hospital room in Naples. Grandpa lay there barely breathing. After several hours they met late in the afternoon with three Doctors. They were unanimous in saying that Grandpa was brain dead and could not control any bodily functions. Possibly an iron lung would keep him breathing for a time.

They made the agonizing decision that he would be best off in a hospice. A representative of the Avow hospice had him transferred there that evening. Young Gerald visited the hospice every day for 13 days before Guzman finally passed away. During the first week, Wallace and Foster often joined him.

Wallace returned to New York City after the first week. When Gerald called him to tell him that Grandpa was gone, as Vice Chairman of the Board of Directors, he asked Barbara Baxter to send out a Notice of a Special Meeting of the Board of Packard Holding Company to take place in the conference room at Packard Village at 2 p.m. the next Tuesday.

By two o'clock on that afternoon, all the directors, except Sam Wallace, had assembled. In addition, Gerald Guzman, Robert Benny and George Foster, who had been invited, were present.

Guzman's three golf buddies huddled in the corner. Shawn was concerned he would lose the use of his Cadillac, Bill bemoaned the fact he would be out the $1,000 meeting fee four or more times a year, and Thomas deplored the possible loss of a free week for himself and his wife to attend the winter meeting at the Doral Country Club and play the Monster course.

Finally, Sam Wallace showed up. It soon became clear that he had imbibed a liquid lunch. Shawn nudged the others, "Looks like Sam is three sheets to the wind."

Bill and Thomas replied, "Better than being drunk as a skunk."

Wallace poured himself a cup of coffee from the carafe on hand, and, after a hiccup, called the meeting to order.

Then he asked Aaron Groom to fill in the Board on the reasons why the late sole stockholder wanted to give the capital stock of the corporation to the Packard Village Foundation.

Groom said that Packard Village was operating at a loss, and based on the report of the actuary, would continue to do so until remedial steps were taken regarding admissions. Accordingly, the sole stockholder might be able to offset his capital gain in another transaction by making a gift of the stock valued at cost to the Packard Village Foundation.

Wallace then asked Robert Benny, who had the responsibility for the CCRCs under the Pickering ownership, to give his views. Benny pointed out that now since the sole stockholder was deceased, it was foolish to value the stock at cost because that would increase the estate tax. It should be valued according to an appraisal, based on the report of the actuary, at a much lower figure to reduce the estate tax.

He further said the news that applicants had a chance to live three extra years would be such a tremendous selling tool that he would recommend that Packard Village be expanded by adding additional independent apartments with new deluxe club houses.

To the surprise of the Board, Wallace then asked the 21 year old Gerald Guzman if he would like to address the

Board in place of his grandfather. The young man thanked the Board for this opportunity and said under the terms of his grandfather's will, he had been advised that he would become the sole owner of the stock of Packard Holding Company as soon as probate proceedings had been completed.

He then thanked Wallace and Foster who had saved enough of his grandpa's speech to make it clear he intended to give the stock to the Packard Village Foundation. He added that he was certain that his grandfather did not mean to deprive his friends of their prerequisites. He went on:

"At the hospice, I sat with Grandpa for thirteen days. Most of the time I was alone, but I thank Sam Wallace and George Foster for their several visits. As Grandpa lay there hardly breathing, each day I studied the legible part of his speech notes. Each day, I touched his hand, tried to wake him up with a funny story and kissed him good night.

"After losing the rest of my family in the Egyptian air crash, he had been wonderful to me. I have had thirteen days to think about what Grandpa would want me to do in the current circumstances.

"First, he would congratulate Barbara Baxter and Aaron Groom on their recent engagement and provide Barbara with a generous pension if she decides to retire as Mrs. Groom.

"Second he would want Sam, Shawn, Bill and Thomas to continue on the Board for three years with their stipend, Cadillacs and a winter meeting at Packard Village.

"Then he would ask the Packard Village Foundation to nominate six qualified residents to the Board to manage Packard Village for ten years for the benefit of both the residents and the staff. To be sure these objectives are obtained he would place the stock in the name of three voting trustees — myself, Sam Wallace and George Foster. If the Foundation meets these objectives for ten years, the voting trust will terminate and the stock revert to the Foundation."

Wallace thanked young Guzman for his generous but prudent proposal and, since the carafe of coffee was now drained, adjourned the meeting, subject to recall, on completion of probate proceedings.

CHAPTER NINE

The Octogenarian

Foster looked at the calendar. It was November 12th, 2020. Foster thought, *It has been more than twenty years since I first came to Packard Village as a spy. In two days Buddy and Penny and a whole bunch of my nieces and nephews are coming to celebrate my ninetieth birthday in the private dining room. They must think I am still rich! They will call on me to speak, what will I say? What have I accomplished? I know that all the retired employees of the State of Connecticut are better off because of my actuarial work. But I also know that after Lucy Barksdale sliced up her arm on the corner of that damned rumble seat, I failed to fill her prescription until after an infection set in.*

When I went over to help Lucy out, she asked me to stay overnight in her large apartment. The first night, I slept in her guest bedroom, I dreamed I had been invited to stay by

Marlene Dietrich – maybe because both had guttural accents or maybe because both had long legs.

The next morning, I mentioned Marlene Dietrich to her, and she immediately broke out into a haunting rendition of Lilli Marleen — how does it go — "underneath the lamplight by the barrack gate, Darling I remember the way you used to wait" — but she sang it in German.

Until she passed away, my new career was that of an aide to a significant other, like many other residents are aides to significant others and sometimes even aides to insignificant spouses!

Should I tell them that my predictions of increased lifespan at Packard Village were spot on? Or mention that scientists find replacing worn out human cells more complicated than those of purple jellyfish? Besides, I'd far rather be a mortal human than live forever as a perpetual purple jellyfish. When I moved here, I did not know that the "Un"affordable Care Act cuts off payments to seniors for hospital stays and cancer treatments at age 76.

Then came Congress, and when China quit buying our bonds, the Government's Ponzi scheme was over. Instead of welching on payments of interest on our bonds, Congress cut social security payments in half.

Then should I mention that many residents run out of funds to pay the monthly maintenance fees, and must rely on the provisions of the Florida Insurance Law under which continuing care communities must provide care so long as it does not exhaust the down payment to the holding company? Of course no place is perfect.

Should I mention the dispute between the duplicate bridge players like myself and the failure of the management to pay the beautiful Belgian Bridge Director to tell us when to "skeep" to the next table? That resulted in most of the men quitting duplicate and forming a male bridge group.

No, I shall talk about the generosity of young Gerald Guzman, who followed through with his grandfather's wish to give the shares of Packard Holding Company to the Packard Village Foundation. And I shall talk about the construction of the luxurious new Club houses and massive residence halls and their decoration with modern art rather than art by residents.

How about the absence of many nostalgic touches such as the grandfather clock and other artifacts from the old club houses? We were fond of them, but they will only be remembered by we who are in the rumble seat of our lives.

No, I'll skip all that. Let me just say that my guests are welcome at Packard Village. I have found it is a wonderful place to live. The food is great, the company full of fun. If you like golf, tennis, croquet or swimming, the courses, courts and pools are here. Art, music recitals and other activities abound. The gym is equipped with as many exercise machines as there are muscles in the human body. If you like nature, the grounds are shaded by stately trees, enlivened with colorful flowers and bushes, and the greenest of grasses. If you like the ocean, you will also enjoy the gentler Gulf.

I'll keep the speech short and invite the guests, who have come to celebrate the 90th Anniversary of my birth, to join me that evening for a walk on the beach to witness the green flash as the sun sets.

THE AUTHOR, Karl
Connell (Jr.), was reared
in the Catskill Moun-
tains along a trout fishing
stream. At five years old,
he played a game of chess
with his father nightly
by the light of a kerosene
lamp. His father won
except on Sundays when
they played for One Dol-
lar. On Sundays he usu-
ally won. Later the author
attended Millbrook School
and Yale College, which he left to join the Army.

After 37 months service, during which 14% of his Squad-
ron lost their lives, he returned to Yale and then Columbia
Law School. He practiced law In New York City with Breed,
Abbot & Morgan, then headed legal affairs for the American Stock Exchange. He moved on to General Counsel of
GAC Corporation in Miami, Florida. He left GAC to join
the Fowler, White Burnett firm there.

In 1990, he retired to his Catskill home and became
embroiled in a seven year battle with New York City over
water rights. Finally settled, the Karl Connell award is
made annually, named for him as a leader in conservation
who helped mediate citizen rights up stream with the New
York City interest in protecting its water supply.